JOHN MICHAEL LAFAUCI II

THE SEASONS OF LIFE

A NOVEL

The Seasons of Life

Visit our website at
www.StillwaterPress.com
for more information.

First Stillwater River Publications Edition

ISBN: 978-1-960505-37-8

1 2 3 4 5 6 7 8 9 10
Written by John Michael LaFauci II.
Illustrated by Cade John LaFauci.
Edited by Joan J. LaFauci.
Cover and interior design by Elisha Gillette.
Published by Stillwater River Publications, Pawtucket, RI, USA.

The Seasons of Life

It has often been said that people come into your life for a reason, a season, or a lifetime. This is a story of a man, the people and animals that came into his life, and how they changed him from what he once was to what he would become. Sometimes, it takes longer for these people to enter your life, and sometimes they stay for a moment, a short time, or a lifetime. In the case of James O'Reilly, it took longer than most for these people to enter his life, but the profound effect, that they would have on him, would be life-changing.

This journey takes place in the 1960s when times were much simpler. Phones were still on the wall with a rotary dial. Television programs still ended at midnight with nothing more than a channel symbol on the screen until morning, when the broadcasting day would begin with the national anthem. Color television was still in its infancy, and those who had a color

TV were considered wealthy or financially reckless. People walked everywhere, and young children spent hours outside playing with little or no supervision by their parents. Most of the businesses in town were family owned except for the A&P food store or Sears and Roebuck.

This slow-paced life made it easy for a man like James to survive without having much contact with others. Without ever being approached to converse, loners such as James were often whispered about by others in town. James was fine with this chilly distance that existed between him and most of the other people in town. He felt proud of his service to his country, so every Fourth of July and Veterans Day, he attended the parades, and every Memorial Day, he made his yearly trip to the cemetery to pay homage to those who had not made it back home after the war. He was a good man who lived a life of solitude and loneliness until certain events changed all that.

To better understand the story, it would make sense to better understand James. He had lived in many places in his life but had never really settled in any of them. He served in the army during WWII. As a teenager he had joined the army and escaped a house riddled with emotional abuse. His Irish Catholic dad was always cruel to both him and his mom, especially when his dad had stopped at the local bar after work for a few cold ones. Luckily, after yet another abusive incident, his mom took him and moved to an uncle's home in a distant town. A quick divorce later and with the assurance that mom was safe and happy, James enlisted in the army and honorably served for four years in Europe. He landed on the beach at Normandy, somehow surviving the onslaught of the Germans who controlled France at the time.

The attack began about one hundred yards from the shore of Omaha Beach. The attack had been named Project Overlord and was the Allies' attempt to defeat the Germans, who had established themselves in France. James was part of the 116th Infantry Division, and was on one of the shallow landing ships that were going to drop the soldiers on Omaha Beach. The day itself was cool, windy, and rainy, somewhat cold for an early June day. The temp was in the forties. The waves were rather rough. and the trip towards the shore was very rocky, causing James and many of the others to get seasick. Most of the soldiers had life jackets on, but, unfortunately, many of them had inflated theirs. This caused them to flip over into the water and drown. Those rangers, who had not bothered to inflate their life jackets, managed to survive this part of the attack. There was bedlam and chaos everywhere around James. The mines that had been put along the beach by the Allies should have detonated before the rangers arrived. They did not, which added to the problems facing the attacking group. This meant that there were very few ditches in which James or his fellow soldiers could hide for cover.

The attack continued for what seemed an eternity. Soldiers around James were drowning, being shot, screaming in pain, and frightened about the fact that they were not going to survive to see another day. At one point, James was shot in his lower leg. The bullet exited out the other side, but he was still bleeding quite a lot. There was blood everywhere. The water near the beach was turning a pinkish-red from all the rangers who had taken a bullet or been fatally shot. For James, it seemed like there were dead bodies everywhere. One of the rangers in his company had taken a bullet and was in a great deal of pain. James managed to grab the soldier by his backpack and somehow drag him to an area on the beach that offered some cover. He, too, was in pain, and, after getting the two of them to cover, James blacked out. Still waiting for reinforcements that were not coming, James and the others in his company were potentially facing a grim fate.

The next time James woke up, he was in a military hospital. The next few weeks, recovering from his wounds and hypothermia, James went in and out of consciousness at the hospital. None of the nurses could tell him much about how long he was passed out on the beach, but somehow, he was rescued and brought to safety. James never knew what happened to the soldier he'd dragged to that area of the beach that apparently saved them both. Operation Overlord lasted about three months and resulted in a significant Allied victory over the Germans. James was not there for the end of the war. He was still recovering in another hospital, this time in the United States. His recovery lasted a few months and involved physical therapy for his leg and counseling for the trauma he had witnessed.

Unlike today, there was no diagnosis of PTSD. Soldiers, who saw unspeakable things, were encouraged to talk about them to therapists. Most, however, went back home and did their best to shut out all that they had seen. Some, like James, were able to survive by blocking out their experiences and not speaking of it. Others found their comfort at the bottom of a bottle and were never again able to live good, productive lives. Over the years that followed, James lost contact with most of the members of his company. Occasionally, he would receive mail inviting him to a reunion of his squadron, but he never went. Better to leave that part of his life buried in the past along with the soldiers who never made it out of there.

Sometime later, James received three medals from the United States government. He was given the

Purple Heart, the Medal of Honor, and the World War II Victory Medal. One of the three medals was given to him for saving the soldier whom he had pulled from the cold, bloody water that day at Normandy. Wanting nothing more to do with that time in his life, James put the three medals away in a small drawer in his bedroom. He did not display them in a frame like many would rightly do. Out of sight and out of mind was the option James chose. With this part of his life put to rest, he was somehow able to get back to a quiet life in his small town. The war had a sobering effect on him. Although he was able to come home and find employment for many years with a local manufacturing plant, he never really overcame the pain of his family life and the horrors of war that he experienced.

Marriage never was a consideration for him. so he made a life for himself while keeping his distance from most of the people with whom he came in contact on a daily basis. Although he was never diagnosed, he probably had some sort of personality disorder, which might have explained his inability to properly interact with others.

Upon his return home from the military, he found a small apartment over the local hardware store that was offered to him by Ted, the owner of the store. Ted was more than happy to rent the space to a single, military veteran, who had very few visitors and was quite the introvert. Ted himself was a former military man, having served about the same time as James. He had been stationed in the Asian theater and would occasionally tell stories of his experiences. James was not so open about his time in Europe. He was just pleased to have this small apartment without any of the typical yard and maintenance issues that come with home ownership. The two men got along well and were a perfect complement to each other.

It was a beautiful, bright, sunny, fall day when James took a walk up the old country road near his apartment. It was the kind of day that you want to enjoy. The temperature had hit the upper sixties, and there was not a cloud in the sky. As he was walking, he came upon a fenced in area that looked a little like a farmyard. It had a rather small building that had been there for a very long time. It was old. and the door was missing. There was a window on the small, barnlike building, but it had no glass in it. The paint on the outside was peeling. and the roof looked like it needed to be fixed. Inside the building was a dirt floor and what appeared to be a pen of some sort for an animal to sleep in. Aside from the old building, the rest of the barnyard was unkempt and looked like it had not been taken care of for some time. James was sad that such an interesting farm had been allowed to fall into such disrepair, but he continued on his morning stroll.

It was then that he noticed a beautiful, brownish horse coming out of the small building, making its way towards him. James waited for the horse to approach him, thinking that perhaps he could get a closer look at this magnificent animal. It just so happened that, in his pocket. he had a fresh apple, which he'd brought with him in case he got a little hungry on his walk. He took out his old army pocketknife. which was clipped to his belt for emergencies like this. Quickly, he cut the apple into four pieces, placed one in the palm of his right hand, and extended his arm over the five-foot fence hoping that the horse would accept his kind gesture and take the apple. Sure enough, the horse very gently took the apple from him and began to chew on it. It didn't take long for the horse to finish off that small piece of apple and the other three pieces the man offered him. This encounter with the horse made James happy; first, because he was in awe of the horse's beauty, and second, because of the quick bond that he seemed to develop with the animal.

Instead of continuing his walk, he stayed at the fence with the horse, stroked his soft brown mane, and scratched his long nose. The horse seemed to totally enjoy his company and never left the fence. When it was time for James to get back home, he bid farewell to the horse, promising to return the next day for another visit. The sudden and somewhat unexpected bond that had developed between the two gave James a warm feeling inside. That night at his home, he couldn't stop thinking about the beautiful horse, wondering who owned him and how he had arrived at this old, unkempt farmyard.

A couple of days passed, and James went about his normal routine of getting coffee and breakfast at the local diner, where he religiously left a very generous tip for his regular waitress Jenna, followed by a stop at the convenience store to pick up his daily newspaper and a pack of gum. The diner had that down-home aroma that was noticeable the second one walked in. The smell of fresh brewed coffee was difficult to ignore, and the odor of cooking oils coming from the kitchen told the tale of a culinary experience that was hard to resist. It was like any other diner out of the '50s and '60s before the inception of McDonald's and all the other fast-food restaurants that followed. They led to the demise of those railcar-shaped diners that had become so popular during and after the wars of the 1920s and '40s. The eatery was full of stools and booths all covered with red vinyl that was cold to sit on in the winter and sticky on the backside in the summer. There was no air conditioning in the place. Any breeze came from opening the doors and windows, which also was an invitation to bugs and an occasional off-course bird. The stools were a combination of seat and amusement park ride. Kids would spin their stools around to their hearts' content, until ordered to cease and desist by an embarrassed parent. There was stainless steel everywhere in the place, shiny and well-polished, which gave the diner a clean look. If the stainless steel wasn't enough there was plenty of chrome which added to the brightness. Most of the booths in the diner had a tabletop jukebox ready to take a person's quarter in exchange for three of the most recent hits of the day. The privilege of playing your favorite song meant that everyone else in the diner had to listen to your choice. There were no earbuds to personalize the music for the listener. It was music for everybody or nobody.

The food at the diner was always passable but far from a culinary delight. Breakfasts of eggs, ham, corned beef hash, and fresh pancakes were always a favorite of the regular customers. James was one of those regulars but changed his order occasionally. He was never the type of customer who came in and ordered "the regular." Jenna would often joke with him about his poor dietary habits, and James would offer a whimsical laugh knowing full well that she was probably right.

There were always fresh pies neatly displayed along the counter. The diner was known to give out the biggest and best pieces of pie in town, so it became a popular item on the menu. Seldom would a customer leave without ordering a piece of apple, blueberry, pecan, or squash pie for dessert, always accompanied by a large scoop of vanilla ice cream.

James usually sat in the same booth in the far corner of the diner. After a while, it almost became an accepted fact that the corner booth was his and his alone. People who went to the diner for breakfast would get there early enough to grab a seat, knowing that when James arrived, he would go directly to the corner booth. On those infrequent occasions when he stopped at the diner for supper, he would sit wherever he could find a vacant seat. Most nights, James cooked up a simple supper at home and dined alone. James was partial to the homemade meatloaf and turkey dinner the rare times he had his evening meal at the diner. He loved that Jenna always managed to add a little extra mashed potatoes or cranberry sauce to his plate.

Over time, he developed a warm feeling for Jenna, the kind of feeling that a father would have for his daughter. He had learned that Jenna was an only child of a single, unmarried mom. Her mom had gotten ill at an early age (forty-five) and spent a short time in a nursing center where she later passed away. She had left Jenna the small Cape-style house where the pair of them had lived. A timely insurance policy in her mom's name had allowed Jenna to pay off the mortgage, leaving her with a minimal amount of monthly bills. The job at the coffee shop, along with her tips, allowed her to survive.

James always remembered Jenna's birthday, Valentine's Day, Christmas, and any other special occasions that allowed him to spoil her with some small monetary gift or something that she had shown an interest in but was unable to afford. Their friendship grew over the years. and the two of them became close friends. Oftentimes, when things at the coffee shop were slow, Jenna and James would chat about things on the news, life dreams, Jenna's cat Whiskers, and James's days in the war. Unlike most young people, Jenna seemed interested in the life, that James had lived, and his experiences in the war. Most employees at the cafe regularly went on to other jobs. Jenna seemed satisfied to stay working as a waitress. The pressure was almost nonexistent, and the regular customers were very friendly to her. She had developed a bond with many of them over time, but none of those bonds were as close as the one she developed with James.

Jenna's outgoing personality was tough to ignore. She was always cheery and patient with the customers. No matter how grumpy they appeared to be, she would always be able to coax a smile out of them. As a young teenager, she had volunteered at the local nursing home as a helper. That job entailed playing games with some of the patients, helping to feed some of those who were unable to feed themselves, and, generally, doing whatever jobs the RNs and LPNs refused to do.

Most young people would have never chosen that type of work, but Jenna's mom had always instilled in her an attitude of giving to others who were less fortunate. Plans to go to nursing school were put on hold when Jenna's mom started to get ill and eventually passed away. In her conversations with James, she often talked about her dreams of becoming a nurse, but would always quickly change the subject, almost as if she knew that her dream was just that, a dream.

One day James decided to take another walk to visit his new animal friend. He stopped back at his apartment, cut up an apple, and made his way up the country road to the farmyard where the horse was being kept. Upon arriving, he was greeted by not only the horse but also a small, plumpish, black pig following the horse around the yard. The two made quite an interesting pair; the big, beautiful horse and this rather dirty, black, and somewhat disgusting looking pig. The funny part was that the two seemed quite at ease with each other. Wherever the horse went, the pig would follow, never missing a beat. When the horse stopped to graze in the little grassy area, the pig would do the same, as if he was mimicking the horse's behavior. James called to the horse and displayed the apple that he had cut up for him. Somewhat quickly, the horse sped to the fence. James gave him a taste of the apple he had so neatly cut. The horse took the first two pieces of apple from James's hand, but on the third offering, the horse deliberately dropped the piece of apple to his side, at which point the chunky little pig scooped it up and quickly devoured it. It was quite evident that the two animals had developed a strong amicable connection with each other and were quite comfortable sharing whatever was given to them.

James laughed, finished feeding the two animals their treat, and began his walk home. On the walk back he couldn't get over the amazing bond that the two animals had with each other, sharing what little treats they were offered and never attempting to get anything extra from the other. This gave James a warm feeling inside, a feeling that would stay with him the rest of the night. Still, the question swirled around in his head. Who owned these animals, and why were they there with what appeared to be little supervision? He fell asleep with that thought racing through his mind.

As often happened, things came up in James's life, so it was a few days before he found the time to take a walk up the road to visit his new friends. As he approached, he noticed a new friend of the horse and pig. This time there was a mangy old sheep whose wool had not been tended to in what appeared to be a very long time. It was dirty, had small twigs caught in it, and in general, looked quite unkempt. Like the little black pig, the sheep followed the horse around the yard as if he was a soldier following his platoon leader. This incident reminded James of his army days, having to follow a platoon leader onto that beach in Normandy. Luckily, the three animals would not face the same fate as the soldiers did on that day. Their reward was an apple or some other treat that James had in his pocket. When the horse stopped to feed on the grass, the pig also stopped, followed by the sheep, forming one peculiar line of farm animals marching around the large pen.

As he had done in the past, James took out the apple from his tote bag and called over to the horse and his friends. On cue, the horse leisurely made his way to the fence, where James stood, and patiently waited for him to hold out his hand with the day's treat. After eating two bites of apple, the horse, in a deliberate manner, dropped the apple from his mouth. It was immediately scooped up by the pig, who gobbled it up and finished with a loud grunt. Without even thinking twice, the horse had again given up his special treat for the benefit of his pig friend. This grand gesture did not go unnoticed by James, who again suddenly felt a warmth in his chest. The mangy old sheep just watched the entire event and proceeded to continue his walk around the yard. It was apparent that the sheep didn't eat apples. Instead, the sheep chose the free hay from the barn.

Days and weeks passed, and James went about his normal routine of breakfast at the diner with Jenna and a stop to pick up his paper and his pack of gum. For some that would seem somewhat boring and repetitive, but for James it was a routine that made him feel safe and comfortable. Almost daily he would make his trip to visit his three new friends at the farm. To some, this partnership might have seemed odd, but to James it was a bond that felt natural. The three animals never judged him. On the contrary, they always seemed happy to see him. Part of that friendliness was probably because James almost always had some type of treat for them. Even on those days when he had forgotten to bring some treats or had come by only on a whim, the trio of animal friends came to the fence to greet him. Still, the question remained as to the whereabouts of the owner and from where the three animals had come.

One day, James's curiosity got the best of him, so he decided to make a visit to the house that was located at the back of the property. Not a real people person, he was very leery as he approached the front porch. What would he say to the person when and if they answered the door? James had never been very good at holding long, meaningful conversations with people. What if he or she came to the door with a weapon and ordered him off the property? What was he going to ask the person when he finally did confront him or her? All these questions ran through James's head as he finally got the courage to ring the bell. It seemed like an eternity as he waited for the response.

Just as he was about to forego this crazy idea and leave, the door opened, and he was face to face with what appeared to be a sweet, elderly lady, no more than five feet tall and weighing a hundred pounds at best. His fears began to wane, and he finally was able to speak. He explained to the little lady that his name was James, and he had been coming by the farm to visit and feed the three animals for quite some time. She seemed quite receptive to him and explained to James that her name was Margaret, and she had seen him on many occasions visiting the animals. The trio of farm animals was from an animal shelter that serviced abandoned livestock. She and her husband had owned a larger farm in their younger years but, upon retiring, decided to buy this smaller farm and bring in older animals for the purpose of giving them a safe and loving place to live out their lives.

Unfortunately, the lady's husband had recently passed, so the woman was left to fend for herself. It was becoming more and more difficult for her to manage the farm and the three animals. This was the main reason for the disrepair of the barn. Her husband had planned to fix the broken window and door on the barn and put a new coat of paint on the structure. Once he became ill, that plan was put on hold. She was getting some assistance from another animal shelter in the next town. They would regularly send over hay and other essentials needed to keep the animals in good health. Even with this little bit of aid, it was becoming more and more of a challenge for Margaret without her husband's help.

Margaret's house was well constructed but required some updating. Not many things were new or even close to modern by 1960s standards. It was quite evident that since her husband had died, Margaret had lost interest in keeping her home neat as a pin, as she said it once had been. What was the point? She had no reason to please anyone. The one person who had mattered to her was no longer alive. There seemed to be a certain sadness in her smile, and although she was very personable to James when he came to the front door, that look of loneliness enveloped her face.

The living room was cute, yet it lacked any newer furnishings. The chair in which Margaret sat needed both new springs and an updated cushion. It sagged when she sat in it as if it wanted to engulf her entire body. James could see that the chair and other furnishings needed to be changed. He felt badly for Margaret and her situation. Here he was a single, middle-aged man, but his apartment was far neater and more modern than hers. There was a distinct mothball odor that one sometimes finds in the homes of older people. All these small imperfections did not bother James enough to cause him to leave Margaret's home. She was so very gracious and hospitable to him when he came to the door unannounced. Surely, that had to count for something.

Margaret showed James around the modest farmhouse. Structurally, it was quite spacious, with the tall ceilings that were the style of the time. There were beautiful crown moldings at the top of the walls bordering the ceilings. Whoever built the home took great pains to make sure that no detail went unnoticed. It seemed a shame that Margaret was in the position of not being able to take care of this architectural gem of a house.

James and Margaret spoke for what seemed like an eternity to him. She encouraged him to stop by and visit the animals whenever he wanted. She offered James some tea, but he politely refused, choosing to end the visit with the promise that he would continue to come and visit his now four new friends. James left that day with conflicting feelings. He loved the charm that the house once possessed but felt sad that Margaret was unable to handle the maintenance of such a great home.

On his way back to the apartment, James felt proud of himself for having a meaningful conversation with another adult other than Jenna. He couldn't wait to tell her about his covert adventure at the small farm.

That night he decided to expand his relationship with the three animals. He would give them names, thus strengthening the new bond he had developed with them. It was easy to come up with names for them. The beautiful horse would be called "Chocolate" for the color of his coat. The pig and the sheep were much easier to name. "Ebony" for the black pig, and "Ivory" for the white, although quite dirty, sheep. James went to bed that night with a great feeling of accomplishment. He had spoken to a stranger at length for the first time in a long time, learned many new things about the mystery farm and its animals, and formalized his relationship with the three animals by naming them. It was a good and productive day for anyone, especially one with James's personality.

James continued his walks to visit Margaret, Chocolate, Ebony, and Ivory. On occasion, he would rake the barn or lay fresh hay for the animals. After a while, James decided that it would be a good idea to put a fresh coat of paint on the barn. It had started to show some wear and needed attention. He resolved to spend a weekend scraping the outside and return the next weekend to paint the outside. Margaret gave James her blessing for him to do the job. She promised to bake him one of her homemade apple pies in payment for his work. Having become friends with James, she knew that any offer of money for the job would have been flatly refused, so baking him the pie was the next best thing.

James was able to get the paint from Ted, his landlord and the hardware store owner, for a discount, so the plan was put into motion. Unbeknownst to James, Jenna had solicited some of her regular customers to show up Saturday to help him with the project. She knew that James, being the proud and private man that he was, would never have asked anyone for help. Early Saturday morning when James showed up at the barn ready to scrape and paint, he was met by ten or so of Jenna's customers ready to help with the painting.

It was hard to describe the look on James's face when these people, with whom he had almost no contact, came with brushes in hand ready to help. Jenna was also there, probably to serve as a buffer for James. It would have been difficult for James to outwardly express his appreciation to any stranger, never mind ten of them. Jenna handled all of that and, with Margaret, provided fresh squeezed lemonade and sandwiches for everyone. The weekend project was a huge success. From that day on, James seemed to be a changed person. He was more forthcoming with the other townspeople, whom he had previously acknowledged with a mere nod or tip of his hat.

Like most things in life, circumstances change, and that was no different for James, Jenna, Margaret, and most of the others in the town. It was now the early 1970s, and box stores began to replace the old "mom-and-pop" operations. The same became true in James's small town. Rumors started to float around that a large building supply/home goods store would be breaking ground in the adjacent town. Many townsfolk eagerly anticipated the addition of such a large business. Along with the revenue, this would probably mean more jobs for the people of the quiet little town. One person not so excited was James's landlord, Ted, the owner of the hardware store. He was older now and had neither the desire nor the energy to deal with this newfound competition that was coming his way.

James, too, could see problems arising. His cozy little apartment would soon be a distant memory if his landlord decided to close up the store and retire to a warmer climate. He began to think about what he would do and where he would go if this all came to pass. These things usually take time, so James knew he did not have to make any rash decisions. It did, however, keep him awake some nights, as he wondered what the future held for him.

Needing to pass the time to keep his mind off the impending move, James continued his regular trips to the farm to visit Chocolate, Ivory, and Ebony. Margaret was starting to slow down a bit, but on occasion, still managed to bake some goodies for James and keep him busy with little chores. That was all going to change.

On a rather cool mid-December day, James made his trip to the farm to put the hay out for the three animals and to check in with Margaret. After tending to the animals, he made his way to Margaret's house to see if she needed anything done around the house or any supplies at the grocery store. James rang the front doorbell and waited patiently for Margaret to answer. She took a little longer to get from her rocker to the door, so it didn't surprise James when she did not respond immediately. Two rings later, James began to get concerned and proceeded to unlock the front door with the extra key that Margaret always left under the front mat. He called out for her but got no response. Making his way to the small sitting room where she loved to sit and knit, he found her, peacefully sitting in her chair, eyes closed, having taken her last breath.

James was not sure how long she had been there, but immediately called rescue services. Finally, over what seemed a lifetime, the paramedics came, checked Margaret's vital signs, and explained to James that Margaret had indeed passed away not long before he had arrived. On the table next to the chair was a cup of tea which was still somewhat warm. It appeared that she didn't have the chance to drink any of the tea but died almost immediately after sitting down. Although saddened by her death, James envied Margaret on her peaceful passing. It was the mirror opposite of those fellow soldiers whom he had fought beside. So many of them had to suffer pain, fear, and abandonment before succumbing to their injuries on that beach. Why couldn't he have saved more of them? James sat and waited with the paramedics while the local undertaker was called to remove Margaret's body from the house. After they left, he sat on the couch thinking about how much he would miss her company and pondering what would happen to the house, the farm, and the animals.

Instead of going directly home, he stopped by the diner to let Jenna know of Margaret's passing and expressed his sadness for her loss. That night, James had a difficult time falling asleep, tossing and turning as he thought about Margaret, his own mom, his upcoming eviction from the apartment, and his three animal friends. The only constant in his life was Jenna. She would somehow make all things right for him. After all, she always had a way of making him feel grounded and safe.

The next few days seemed like a blur for James. There were no living, known relatives of Margaret to be contacted for the funeral arrangements. In what was a bit of a surprise to James and the others who knew Margaret, she had prepaid and preplanned her final arrangements, making things somewhat easier for the funeral director. The service was small, attended by only about twenty-five or so local townspeople. Burial was in a plot at the local cemetery, where Margaret's husband had previously been interred. After the service, James and Jenna went back to the diner, shared a coffee together, and spoke of how wonderful Margaret had been to James and the others in town with whom she had come in contact while living there.

Although there was nothing in writing obligating him to do so, James took it upon himself to go to the farm daily and make sure that the animals were properly taken care of. He paid for the delivery of hay for his three animal friends and made sure that the vet came by to check on Chocolate, Ebony, and Ivory. Chocolate was the one who concerned James and the vet the most. He was getting older and had some signs of Equine Cushing's disease and colic. These two health concerns were often found in horses as they aged, so James and the local vet were diligent in checking on Chocolate.

One day while James was at the farm tending to the animals, a neatly clad gentleman approached the barn. He didn't appear to be anyone whom James recognized, but James, using his newly discovered outward personality, quickly greeted the man with a hearty handshake, introducing himself to the stranger. The gentleman explained to James that he was the lawyer for Margaret's estate, and he was looking for James for the purpose of informing him that Margaret had listed him in her will. James was a bit taken aback by this news but decided that Margaret had probably found it in her heart to leave him something for all the work he had done for her around the farm.

He almost dropped to his knees when the lawyer informed him that Margaret had left specific directions for the lawyer to sign over the entire farm, with all its land, to James. Along with the farm, she had put into trust a rather large sum of money for the maintenance of the farm and the three animals. James was at a loss for words, which was not at all unusual since he still was not the greatest conversationalist. After a few signatures, James was assured by the lawyer that he was now the sole owner of a farmhouse, a barn, and three farm animals. James tried to temper his excitement in front of the lawyer.

Once the lawyer had departed James let out a large howl of joy, scaring the three animals who had made their way to the fence to see what was going on between the two men. The property transfer from Margaret to James could not have come at a more opportune time. As was expected, the big box store broke ground for the building, and James's landlord notified him that he would, indeed, be closing and relocating to a warmer retirement community in the South.

James immediately knew what he had to do. His first stop would be the diner to tell Jenna what had just occurred and then inform her that he would be funding her dream to go to nursing school. James always had a nest egg put aside for any unplanned emergencies, but now he could use this newfound wealth to help another person realize her dreams. Jenna was ecstatic when James gave her the news. James assured her that all her school obligations would be met and that she could start her studies at the beginning of the next term. There was a program at the local college that was set up in such a way as to enable nursing students to get their degree in twenty-four months. Jenna would finally be able to realize her dream of becoming a nurse. The young lady, who was solely responsible for bringing James out of his shell, was now going to be repaid by that same man.

The following week James and Jenna drove to the college and filled out all the forms to ensure that Jenna could start the following term. They made a stop at the college bookstore and picked up some of the books for the introductory courses Jenna would be taking. It had been quite a while since Jenna had done much schoolwork, so getting a head start on the reading would be a prudent idea. With papers filled out, tuition paid, and books in hand, the two friends made their way back to the town. The excitement coming from the two of them could hardly be contained. They smiled and laughed for the entire ride back, now getting ready for a new chapter in their lives.

Those twenty-four months flew by, and before long, Jenna was graduating from nursing school with the promise of a job at a local hospital.

As is usually the case, life went back to some sort of normalcy. James moved into the farmhouse which Margaret had left to him. Little by little, he did some upgrades in order to make the home more suitable to his lifestyle. He became quite comfortable in his new home. At the end of the day, it was not unusual to find James sitting in his Adirondack chair on the porch, enjoying the beautiful sunsets that made their way past the mountains to the west. Although they were getting on in years, the three animals. that he had inherited, kept their daily routines in check. Chocolate recovered from a minor bout with equine colic, and Ebony and Ivory did a lot more resting rather than walking around the fenced in area that had been their home for close to ten years. Times were pretty good for James.

He would often reflect on how life had thrown him a few curveballs and how he had been able to navigate through most all of them. People entered his life at different times, some staying for longer than others, but all of them having a profound effect on him. Occasionally, James could feel a tear welling up in his eyes as he thought about his mother, who had to deal with a lousy marriage only to escape it and live a somewhat happy life. He thought about the men he had fought alongside in the war, many of whom never came home. That special weekend when Jenna enlisted the help of the townspeople to assist James with the barn painting made its way into James's thoughts. It had been quite an eventful and interesting life for James.

One morning when James was out doing some of his daily chores—raking the barn, feeding the three animals, changing out the hay bales, and giving Chocolate his medicine—he began to feel dizzy and decided it would be wise to go to the house and sit for a bit. After resting some, he began to feel better and continued with his normal daily routine. His trips to the diner had become less and less frequent with Jenna now working at the hospital. There wasn't anyone at the diner with whom he could share his stories, and a quiet breakfast could be had at home in the privacy of his own kitchen. After a midmorning cup of coffee on the porch, James went in for a short nap. The short nap wound up lasting longer than expected, so it wasn't until midafternoon that James awoke. He felt okay and spent the rest of the day reading the paper and watching some news channel on which he had become hooked.

The next morning, not long after waking up, James began to feel dizzy again. Not wanting to take any chances, he called his primary doctor and was able to get an appointment for later that morning. The doctor ran a few tests in the office and suggested that James go to the hospital for some more intensive testing. He wasn't quite sure what James was dealing with but wanted to be sure that he did a complete analysis regarding James's diagnosis. A few days later, with a little assistance from Jenna at the hospital, the test results came back. James was suffering from a leaky valve in his heart, which was causing the dizziness. The doctors would have to perform a procedure to correct the issue. It would involve one or possibly two days in the hospital, but the doctor was confident that James would be able to go home to continue his recovery. Jenna made sure that all the incidentals were taken care of at the hospital, and James was released after a two-day stay.

Against James's insistence, Jenna moved into the spare room in the farmhouse to make sure that he followed all the doctor's post-op orders. Although James was cranky and hesitant to agree with this temporary living arrangement, deep down inside, he was tickled pink to have his best friend staying with him. They would be able to resume their great heart-to-heart talks that James had missed since Jenna started her job at the hospital.

Sometimes things take longer than expected. Such was James's recovery. He had a difficult time doing some of the normal things that had always come easy to him. He found himself getting tired quicker than usual. This made it more and more challenging to take care of the animals, clean the barn, and haul bales of hay into the farmyard. He couldn't constantly be asking Jenna to take on a more active role on the small farm. She already was stretched thin doing her hospital job and then coming home to look after him. The feeling of helplessness and dependence was gnawing away at James, causing his recovery to take longer. Stress can do a number on the mind and body. Jenna and James decided that it was in the best interest of both of them to have someone come in for a few hours a day to take some of the pressure off Jenna and give James the attention that he needed to properly recover.

Through a coworker, Jenna was able to contact a nurse who was looking for a few hours a week to supplement her pension. Three days later, the nurse was working at the house. Those four hours a day of outside help made all the difference in the world for Jenna and James. The two of them became refreshed both emotionally and physically. In addition to the nurse, James was able to find a young high school student who was looking for a part-time job. He came to the farm after school and made sure the animals were fed and the barn area was properly maintained. Everything seemed to be going along smoothly again for a while.

James, however, was still somewhat weak from the surgery and was beginning to feel frustrated with his inability to do the things that he had always done. Being an independent person his whole life, James had difficulty accepting all the help being provided. Jenna could see how it was starting to wear on him and tried her best to keep a cheery, light mood when they were together. Sometimes that worked, while other times it was as if her attempts failed.

With Jenna spending more and more time at the house looking after James and less time at her own home, it seemed foolish for her to keep a separate residence. James's farmhouse was plenty big enough for the two of them, so on many occasions she had stayed in the guestroom. They mutually agreed to sell Jenna's house and have her move into the farmhouse with James. Upon setting up this arrangement, they had a lawyer prepare a legal document that gave equal ownership of the house and the adjoining property to Jenna and James. The two of them discussed this arrangement at length. They were very hesitant to take a chance on ruining what had become a wonderful relationship. Money and family can cause problems. Even though they were not blood relatives, their relationship had flourished into a strong bond that had survived the test of time.

With the papers drawn up, Jenna proceeded to move into the house. The house that her mom had left her sold quickly, so she moved all her belongings into the larger farmhouse. Thus began the next chapter in the lives of these two people.

Life on the farm was peaceful and quiet. Jenna took her normal shift at the hospital, and James managed to do what few chores he was physically able to accomplish. Jenna was now in her late thirties and had resigned herself to the prospect of living her life unmarried. She was so busy with all the responsibilities in her life that dating and marriage were things for which she had little time. It wasn't so much that Jenna was against marriage, just that by the time her shift at the hospital was done, she was too tired to get dressed up to go out on a date. She much preferred to go home, get into some comfy sweats, and watch a movie or show with James. Most nights, James would wind up falling asleep before the show even ended.

In respect to our lives, time is an odd concept when we ponder it. As a youth, time goes by with the speed of a snail. With children, days never seem to end, and tomorrow seems light-years away. Everything is about the present. During our adolescent years, we can hardly wait for those milestone birthdays (sixteen, eighteen, twenty-one) to arrive. The older we get, the faster life seems to pass. James had gone through this progression and now found himself on the descending side of life's mountain. By most standards he had lived a good life and was pleased with what he had accomplished. He felt no regrets for what he had done or what he had failed to do. His proudest accomplishment was helping Jenna achieve her dream of becoming a nurse. He had given her a comfortable home in which to live and had provided her with the means by which to live her adult life.

Their life of sharing the house and each other's company went on for a little over a year. James would make his daily trip out to the barnyard to feed the animals. The three animals always seemed happy to see him and always willingly approached him with the hope of getting one of those special treats which they expected. On those days when James felt too weak to go out, Jenna would always make sure that Chocolate, Ebony, and Ivory got their apple and fresh hay.

As the year passed, James's visits to the barn became less and less frequent. He knew he was becoming weaker and let Jenna know that his time with her was fleeting. She always dismissed the thought, telling him that he was much too cranky to die and would probably outlive everyone else in town. Deep down inside, she knew he was right, and prepared herself for what was to come. When he finally passed away on that cold, snowy day, James was at peace with everything around him. Jenna was there just as she had always been. There were no tears from either of them at the end. Although never a big churchgoer, James had made his peace with God and directed Jenna how to handle the funeral arrangements. Because of his service to his country, he was buried at the local veterans' cemetery with full military honors. There was no fanfare after the service. The few townspeople, with whom he had become close, attended the funeral. One by one, they expressed their condolences to Jenna, offering to help her with anything she needed. At the end of the day, Jenna returned to the farmhouse, put a few logs on the fire, sat in silence for the rest of the evening, and finally fell asleep on the couch of which she had become so fond. The only thing missing was her dear friend.

Jenna knew she had to get back to the living. James would have been upset with her if she moped around the house feeling sorry for herself. With those thoughts in mind, she returned to the hospital after taking off a few personal days. Getting back to work was the remedy that she needed. She threw herself into her work, taking on extra shifts and volunteering to serve on a nurses' board at the hospital. Things back at the farm were put into motion. Jenna was able to contact a local rescue facility, which agreed to take Chocolate, Ebony, and Ivory and give them a home to live out their twilight years.

One day at the hospital, about a year after James's death, Jenna met Daniel, a middle-aged widowed doctor who was looking for someone to help him run a clinic he was starting. Previously, they had connected with each other at one of the meetings Jenna had attended in her position as a member of the nurses' board. The clinic would be partially funded by a grant from the state and would service those people who could not afford to get the medical help they needed. The pay was less than what Jenna was making, but money was no longer an issue for her. She had put the money from the sale of her mom's house into an account at the bank and had not spent any of it. James had taken care of most all the bills connected to the running of the farm, so most of Jenna's pay went into the bank or was used for whatever personal things she wanted. She agreed to take the job offer and went to work with Daniel at the clinic.

They became close friends, followed by a short romantic courtship, and finally the two married. Both had a special place in their hearts for their two previous losses. Daniel had married his high school sweetheart; he'd gone to the same college as her, and married her when he finished his internship. Jenna, although never having married, would always feel a special love for James. He had given her a chance to achieve her dream and showed her what it meant to care deeply about another person. There was no whirlwind romance. Jenna and Daniel were at that age when children were not a consideration. Dates for Jenna and Daniel usually consisted of a nice meal at their favorite restaurant. Often, the two would see a movie, complete with a large tub of buttered popcorn. They ran the clinic and spent most of their free time sitting on the front porch at the farm enjoying those beautiful sunsets that Jenna and James had anticipated every night.

Not long after the two married, Daniel received news that his dad had passed away. He had always been close to his dad, even if work managed to keep him a short distance away. Daniel had visited regularly to check on his health and well-being, although his sister was their dad's primary caregiver since she lived closer.

After the funeral and cleaning out his dad's house, Daniel and Jenna were left with a few boxes of old mementos and photos that Daniel's dad had kept over the years. One rainy night, when there was no sunset to enjoy, Jenna and Daniel decided to go through the boxes to see what interesting things they could find. Most of the boxes contained papers that were useless. There were quite a few old photos and some of the military medals that Daniel's dad had kept. Many of the pictures were of his military days with members of his platoon. Sometimes the names were on the back of the photos, but often the number of names did not match the number of people in the photo. After all, many of these connections were short-lived. In many cases, the names were known only by the label on the front of their uniform.

One picture that Jenna was looking over was of Daniel's dad with another soldier next to him. On the back of the picture was an inscription that read, "James O'Reilly and me in boot camp." The date on the picture indicated that it had been taken months before the Normandy invasion. Jenna dropped the picture on the floor. "James O'Reilly," the same James O'Reilly to whom Jenna had grown so close? She immediately showed the picture to Daniel and insisted they do some research to determine if what she was seeing in the picture was true.

Doing their due diligence with the aid of military records, Jenna and Daniel were able to find out that James and Daniel's dad had indeed served in the same unit at the same time. Without a doubt, it was James standing beside Daniel's dad in the picture. They also concluded that, upon further study, it was James who had saved Daniel's dad on that terrible day in Normandy. The two had been taken to different army hospitals and had never managed to connect after the war ended. A new sense of closeness came over Jenna and Daniel at the realization of the connections they shared. It was as if everything that had happened was meant to be. James saves Daniel's dad; Jenna meets

James; James visits Margaret's farm and connects with the three animals; Jenna meets Daniel.

While sitting on the porch enjoying one of those majestic sunsets, Jenna realized what James had discovered years earlier. People come into your life at different times and for different reasons. She had been a part of these connections with James, Margaret, and now Daniel. Some for a reason, some for a season, and others for a lifetime. All these relationships mold our lives. Hopefully, many of them change us for the better. In the case of James and Jenna, they most certainly did.

About the Author

John LaFauci earned his bachelor's degree from Rhode Island College in Sociology and his master's degree in Secondary School Administration from Providence College. As such, he worked as a History teacher in the Warwick School System for 20 years and a Middle School Administrator in North Providence for 6 years. He was a high school soccer coach at Pilgrim High School and Burrillville High School. In 2008, he was honored in Rhode Island and Washington D.C. as Rhode Island Vice Principal of the Year. He also served on the Smithfield School Committee for four years. He has been married to his wife Joan LaFauci, a former English teacher in Cranston for 28 years. They have been married for 52 years. They have two grown children, Brian LaFauci, a self-employed businessman, who owns a personal consulting company and a real estate holding company. His daughter, Ashlee Barton is a school psychologist in the Smithfield School Department and owns her own spin and fitness studio.

This is his first attempt at a short novel, having written numerous short articles for local magazines. When not writing, John enjoys golf, tennis, and pickleball. Joan and John have done extensive traveling, always looking to broaden their horizons and discover new and interesting places and things. In his free time, he is kept busy attending the athletic events of his two grandchildren, Ava and Cade LaFauci.

www.ingramcontent.com/pod-product-compliance
Lightning Source LLC
La Vergne TN
LVHW010945110826
845149LV00013B/2760

* 9 7 8 1 9 6 0 5 0 5 3 7 8 *